HOW TO LIGHT

your

dragon

Didier Lévy   Fred Benaglia

HOW TO LIGHT
your
dragon

Thames & Hudson

Has your pet dragon's fire GONE OUT?

· · · · · · · · · · · ·

don't worry. THERE MUST BE A WAY TO RELIGHT HIM!

PERHAPS SOMETHING'S BLOCKING HIS FLAMES

Try lifting up his back legs AND GIVING HIM A GOOD SHAKE

MAYBE HE NEEDS A NEW SPARK!
A GOOD WAY TO MAKE A SPARK IS TO FIND A FEATHER DUSTER

AND TICKLE YOUR DRAGON

TICKLE HIS FEET ...

UNDER HiS ARMS ...

AND THE **TiP** OF HiS NOSE.

STiLL NOTHiNG?

TAKE YOUR DRAGON SHOPPING.
THEN SHOW HIM THE LATEST OVENS
AND SING THEIR PRAISES.

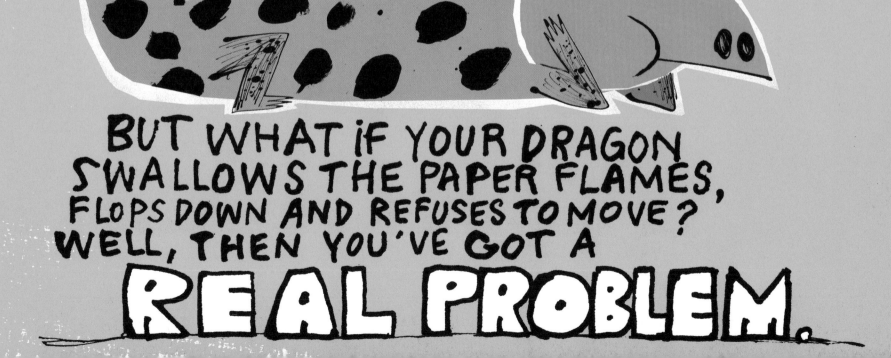

AND ALL THE ADVENTURES YOU'VE HAD TOGETHER.

Translated from the French *Comment rallumer un dragon éteint*

First published in the United Kingdom in 2019 by
Thames & Hudson Ltd, 181A High Holborn,
London WC1V 7QX

This paperback edition first published in 2020

Original edition © 2016 Éditions Sarbacane, Paris
English translation rights arranged through La Petite Agence, Paris
This edition © 2019 Thames & Hudson Ltd, London

British Library Cataloguing-in-Publication Data
A catalogue record for this book is available from the British Library

ISBN 978-0-500-65233-6

Printed and bound in Malaysia

To find out about all our publications, please visit
www.thamesandhudson.com. There you can
subscribe to our e-newsletter, browse or download our
current catalogue, and buy any titles that are in print.